MIKE HIGGS

MOONBIRD

A DRAGON BOOK

GRANADA

London Toronto Sydney New York

D1312972

It was night time in Purple
Woods. Hooter the Owl sat in
his tree and blinked. Suddenly
a small, silvery-white creature
came gliding down a moonbeam
towards him.

The silvery-white creature landed at the end of the
moonbeam under Hooter's tree. Hooter flew down.
'Who-ooo are you?' hooted Hooter.

'I'm a moonbird,' answered the silvery-white creature.
'When I hatched on the moon there was no one there.
So I flew down to earth to look for other moonbirds.
Have you seen any of my family?' he asked, sadly.

Hooter blinked his big,
round eyes.
'I have never seen a
creature like you in my
life before,' he said,
and flew up to his tree.
'I must look somewhere
else,' thought Moonbird.

Moonbird flew and flew.
At last he came to
the end of the land
and there below him
he saw the wide ocean.
A small boat with two
sailors on board was
bobbing on the waves.

'Have you seen a creature like me in your lives
before?' Moonbird asked, hopefully.
'To be sure we have, laddie,' said the fat sailor.
'It was on an island far from here,' said the thin one.

'We'll take you there,' said the sailors.
'Hop aboard, shipmate.'
Soon after the sky grew black and the sea grew rough.

Moonbird was very frightened. He held tight to
the boat. The sailors held tight to the wheel. The
lightning flashed, the sea foamed and the wind howled.
Suddenly a huge shape loomed in front of them.
'It's the island,' yelled the thin sailor.

But as they came nearer to the huge shape they saw
that it was not an island. It was a gigantic,
scaly green monster with an enormous, open mouth.

They could not escape.
The boat sailed right
into the enormous mouth,
and the gigantic monster
swallowed them,
in one gulp, down into
its dark, dark
insides.

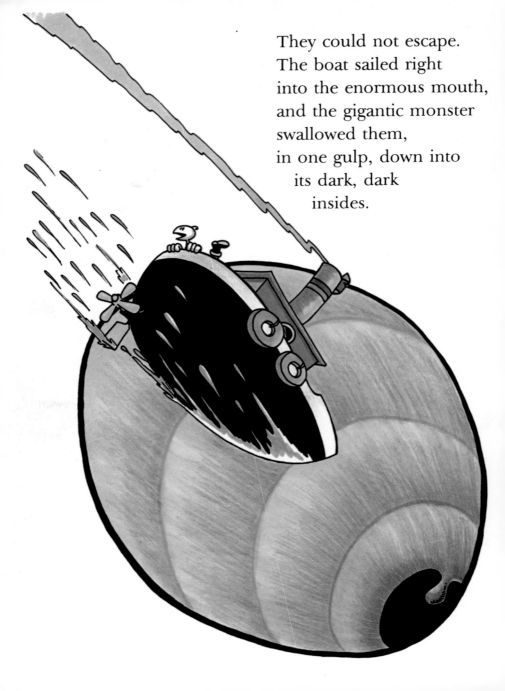

'Light the lantern,' whispered the thin sailor,
'so we can see where we are.'

The monster's stomach was a vast cave. All around
lay the wrecks of ships the monster had swallowed
before. The three friends bravely set out to explore.

They peered through a hole in the hull of one of the
wrecks and saw an old treasure chest.
'Shine a light, there,' said the fat sailor.

They climbed into the wreck. But they hadn't seen a
fierce octopus lurking in the shadows. As they
crept along, it stretched out its tentacles
and grabbed them. 'Help! Help!' they shrieked.

Moonbird forgot his fear. He flew at the octopus
and landed on its head.
Ferociously he pecked and furiously he flapped.
The octopus was so angry that it let go of the sailors.

But it could not catch Moonbird.
He flew round and round the octopus's head until
the creature was so dizzy it got its tentacles in a twist.

The three friends fled back to their boat.
'We must escape from here,' panted the thin sailor.
'We need a plan,' said Moonbird.

'What if we build a fire?
The smoke will make the
monster cough and we'll be
coughed out.'
'Bright bird,' said the thin
sailor.
They collected driftwood
and lit a fire. Then they
got in their boat and waited.

Smoke swiftly filled the monster's
stomach and swirled up its neck.
The choking fumes made
the monster give a great cough
and the little boat shot up its throat,
and out of its enormous mouth.

As the boat settled back on the green water
they were just in time to see the monster's huge
tail vanish beneath the waves.
'Land, ahoy!' shouted the thin sailor. There on the
horizon was the very island they had set out to find.
Right in the centre of the island was a mountain.
Moonbird felt very excited. Perhaps this was the
place where he would find his family.
'You can fly the last few yards, my lad, just in
case this is another monster,' said the thin sailor.

Moonbird thanked
the sailors and
said goodbye.
Then he flapped
his wings, rose
boldly into the air
and flew towards the
shore. He landed on
a hot, sandy beach.

He looked up through the trees to the mountain.
It had a strange, flat top. 'Maybe there is a crater
inside,' squeaked Moonbird, excitedly.
'This could be the place where my people come
when they are on the earth.' He soared up through
the trees towards the top of the mountain.

He flew to the rim of the crater and peered inside.
And there, row upon row upon row, were the nests of

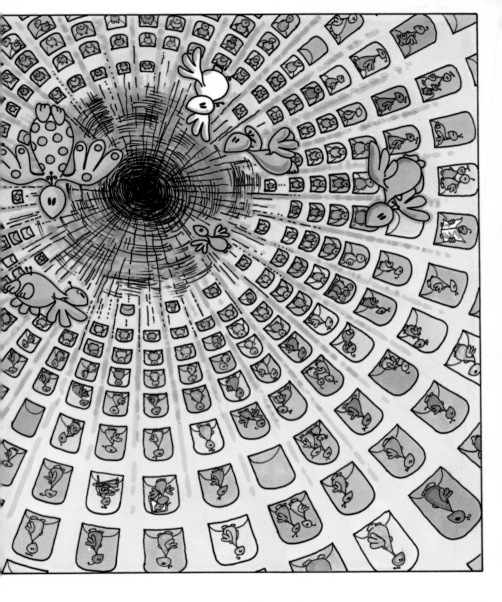

the moonbirds. 'Yipee! I've found them,' sang Moonbird,
and he flew round and round the inside of the volcano.

His mother and father were overjoyed to see him.
His brothers and sisters crowded round him, bouncing
and cheeping with happiness.
'We're on holiday!' they all shouted at once. 'You
were only an egg when we left so you couldn't come.'

The young moonbirds were so glad to be together that they flew straight up out of the volcano and into the bright, blue sky. Round and round they flew swooping and looping in the hot, tropical sunshine.

In the evening
Moonbird's father called
his family together.
'The moon is full and
our flock is planning
to return home tonight.
We must go with them,
my chicks,' he said.
Moonbird felt sad.
He did not want to
leave the bright,
warm earth so soon.

That night the whole flock flew off into the bright moonbeams on their way to the moon. All except Moonbird. He stood alone on a rock and waved.

'Goodbye,' he called. 'Goodbye . . .'bye . . .eyee,'
echoed back from the black sky.
When the very last moonbird had vanished into the
sky, Moonbird flew up from the island and turned
towards the east. The first warm glow of the rising
sun was just shining over the ocean.
'The earth is a fine, exciting place,' he thought.
'What on earth would I do on the moon!'